⇢ The Big Chair ⇠

The
Big Chair

A Story of Grief
& Discovery

By

Beth Rotondo

Illustrated by Victoria Krassa

STILLPOINT PRESS
Weymouth, Massachusetts

THE BIG CHAIR
A Story of Grief & Discovery
By Beth Rotondo
Illustrated by Victoria Krassa

Published by Stillpoint Press
157 Mt. Vernon Rd. East
Weymouth, MA 02189
bethrotondo@verizon.net

Cover & Book Design by
Arrow Graphics, Inc., Watertown, Massachusetts
info@arrow1.com
Printed in China

ISBN: 978-0-9760165-1-9
Library of Congress Control Number:
2007904789

→ Dedication ←

*To the children who yearn for a
Mrs. Seasons in their lives.*
BR

For Gus and Lucy
VK

✦ Acknowledgments ✦

I am grateful to my colleagues, friends, and family who have offered their "Big Chairs" to me in support and love.

Contents

◇ Anna ◇

Hello, my name is Anna. I live in a town called Centerville. I have an older brother named Tom, who likes to tease me a lot. I don't think he wants to be mean but sometimes it feels like it. One time he hid behind a door in the attic and when I came upstairs, he yelled boo so loud I thought I would never stop shaking. I also have a sister Susan who is older than me. She likes to play house. She always wants to be the mom so I'm always the little kid who has to do what she says… "be a good girl now and do this for me."

My best friend's name is Julie. She is in the same grade as me. We like to play computer games. We also like to draw. I like to use pencils to draw my pictures. I like to see all the different shades I can get with my pencil. Julie likes to use colored pens. She likes to draw houses, farms, skies with different clouds and rainbows. I live in a pink house with a nice yard. It has pretty flowers in it. I have my own bedroom. I like to go there and play or just be by myself.

A few months ago something happened in our family. Sometimes I find it hard to say this out loud—maybe it won't be true if I don't say it. Maybe I'll whisper it to you—

my mom died. I can hardly believe this is true. It feels so weird to say this. I don't know why this happened to me. Did I do something wrong? Am I the only one in my school whose mom died? Who do I talk to about this? My brother just tells me to be quiet. My sister tells me everything will be all right but I don't believe her. Nothing feels all right now. Nothing is the same.

And my Dad. I haven't told you about my Dad yet. He's so different now. He seems like he is not really here—like he is busy or something. I can't talk to him because I don't want to upset him. He looks sad a lot.

Mrs. Seasons lives down the street from us in a small white house. She has lived alone for a while. Her husband died. They never had any children. She always takes walks around the neighborhood. My Dad helps her out with the big things outside, like cutting branches or shoveling the driveway. My mom used to bring Mrs. Seasons some flowers from our garden. She is taller than my mom, always has her gray hair twisted up on the back of her head and always wears these big brown shoes. They have hooks on them that you put laces through. You would never wear a dress with them. It would look really bad. She loves to buy us jelly donuts and gives them to us when we are outside playing. Her favorite donut is grape. My favorite is cherry, although these are very hard to find. My mom's favorite was strawberry.

A few weeks ago I was playing jump rope in front of Mrs. Seasons' house. Not many kids play jump rope but I still like to play it. Mrs. Seasons came outside and watched me jump. One time I jumped 57 times without missing. This time I jumped 11 and missed. I felt real bad, like I couldn't do anything right. Nothing was right and I felt alone, all by myself. Mrs. Seasons walked over to me, took my hand and asked if I wanted some cookies.

"Let's go in the house and you can sit in my big chair. It's a great place to snuggle into."

I took Mrs. Seasons' hand and walked with her into her white house. I called my sister and told her where I was. She said to come back home by 6:00. Mrs. Seasons took the cookies from a tin on the shelf in her kitchen. I took the chocolate chip one and she took the peanut butter cookie. Her kitchen was bigger than ours. There was a table in the corner. I thought we would sit there but she said, "No, let's eat cookies in the living room."

There was a couch and two chairs and I knew right away which chair was the big chair. Mrs. Seasons walked me to the big chair. I sat down and fit myself into the corner. I felt it was too big for me but Mrs. Seasons said to give it time.

"Sometimes things feel different after we sit with them for awhile," she said. I ate my cookie and Mrs. Seasons ate hers. She made good cookies. We talked about a few things that day. I can't remember what they were. But I do remember how I felt. I felt that anything I said to Mrs. Seasons was OK, even when I didn't feel it was OK.

I spent many days sitting in the big chair at Mrs. Seasons' house. I asked a lot of questions that had been bothering me and I said a lot of things that I had been too afraid to say out loud. I want to tell you about these meetings in the big chair. Maybe you won't feel so alone or so afraid if this happens to you.

⇢ Laughter ⇠

Mrs. Seasons and I agreed that anytime I needed to eat a cookie and sit in the big chair, I could knock on her door. I wasn't totally sure about this but thought I would give it a try one day. I was having another one of those awful days—nothing was going right and everybody was bothering me. I walked over to Mrs. Seasons' house and rang the doorbell. It was a little round cat's head. Its nose was the ringer. I thought it was cute. Mrs. Seasons opened the door, her gray hair up like it always was. She smiled that nice warm smile and invited me in. Soon I was sitting in the big chair, eating my chocolate chip cookie. She was sitting in the chair next to the couch, eating her peanut butter cookie. I talked about school, my favorite subjects and favorite teacher.

"It's Mrs. Snyder. I like her because she never yells at us. She makes school fun".

"I'm glad school is fun for you," Mrs. Seasons said.

I was happy Mrs. Seasons said that.

"Sometimes I'm not sure if I should be happy," I said.

Mrs. Seasons looked very closely at me now. I wondered if I should say anything else.

"What do you mean, Anna? Why shouldn't you be happy?"

"I don't know. Sometimes I feel real sad, like nothing will be right again. But sometimes, like when I'm drawing my pictures or eating ice cream, I feel OK, like nothing is wrong. I get real confused. My dad and sister don't play with me like they used to. Maybe people think I don't love my mom if I'm playing outside and having fun."

Mrs. Seasons didn't say anything right away. I wondered if I said something wrong. Then she said something I never forgot.

"You can be happy and sad, Anna. You don't have to choose. It's like nature. There is daytime and nighttime—there is a sun and a moon, morning and night. We don't choose what feelings we feel. They just are, like day and night, sun and moon. They come and they go. Try not to worry about what other people may think. You are the only one who knows your heart. Trust it and share it with only those who love you."

I didn't understand all of what she said but somehow I felt it was important to remember—trust my heart and share it with only those who love me.

⇒ Leaves ⇐

One day Mrs. Seasons and I were in the back yard. She was raking the leaves off her porch.

"They make the porch slippery if I leave them there, Anna."

"Why," I wondered.

"Because when the leaves get wet, they begin to get soggy and change to something very soft. After a while, they don't even look like leaves anymore. They eventually turn into dirt. They give the earth a gift."

This sounded interesting as well as

weird. I started to look more closely at the leaves on the porch to see if I could see any change taking place. I started kicking them around with my feet and they just moved wherever I kicked them. But when I got to the bottom layer of the pile, I could see what Mrs. Seasons was talking about. I could almost see the shape of the leaves on the porch.

"Look at this," I said, pointing to these dark shapes of leaves that had fallen on the porch. "Is this what you mean?"

"Yes," Mrs. Seasons said. "All of nature leaves something for us to wonder and discover."

Mrs. Seasons said one of those things I didn't understand but knew it was important.

We finished raking the leaves and went inside for some cookies…our favorite ones, of course. I was sitting in the big chair, looking outside at the leaves.

"Mrs. Seasons, when people die, do they leave gifts for us to wonder about?"

Mrs. Seasons didn't wait to answer this question.

"Oh yes, Anna. Sometimes you can see the gifts they leave. They are right in front of you, clear as a bell. And other times you have to look a little longer to find them."

"What gifts did my mom leave?" I asked.

"Your mom left many, Anna. You are one of her most beautiful gifts. She loved you and was proud of you. Everyone that your mom knew has something from her."

"What did she leave you?" Anna asked.

"She left me her smile. Her smile makes me feel warm inside. I knew she cared about me. Your mom was special, Anna."

I was feeling like I wanted to cry but also happy that my mom was my mom.

"Look for the gifts from your mom, the special things she's done for you, the special things she said to you, the many ways she made you feel loved."

Later that day, I was sitting on my bed, thinking about the things I talked about with Mrs. Seasons. I was wondering what gifts my mom left me. I walked to the mirror and looked very closely at myself. My dad said I have his nose. My mom always said I have her eyes and the color of her hair. Is this what Mrs. Seasons was talking about? My mom also said I have her giggle. "It's contagious," she would say. She would always call me Anna Banana when she wanted to hear me giggle and then she would giggle and then both of us would be giggling all over the place. We had so much fun.

I reached out and touched my face in the mirror, outlining my eyes and my hair, tracing one path that connects my mom and me, hoping to discover others along the way.

→ My Book ←

One time I was sitting in the big chair at Mrs. Seasons' house. It was cold outside and I didn't feel like playing. I had finished my cookie and was looking out the window. Almost all the leaves had fallen off the trees.

"Mrs. Seasons," I said.

"Yes, Anna."

Mrs. Seasons was looking at some pictures she had on the table in front of the couch. They were pictures of all the trips she and her husband took together.

"Mrs. Seasons, will I ever see my mommy

again? I think about this a lot. Will she look like she always did? Will she recognize me if she sees me again when I am older or grown up? I can't believe I'll never see her again. I miss her so much. She would read stories to me in my bed at night. She would lie down right next to me. Sometimes I would read to her if she felt tired. She liked when I read to her. I wonder if she's flying in the sky somewhere. I feel so sad when I think of her not seeing me. I just want a hug from her."

I started to cry a little. I felt funny crying in Mrs. Seasons' living room.

Mrs. Seasons slowly walked from her chair to the couch near the big chair. She still had the pictures in her hand.

"It's OK, Anna. I sometimes cry when I think of not seeing my Frank anymore.

There are days I'm just sad. We used to have such fun together. He had this cute smile. When I'm feeling real sad, I look at the pictures and remember all the fun times we had. I cry and laugh, sometimes at the same time. I don't know, Anna, if I'll ever see Frank again. But I do know that I am awfully glad I met him. I try to remember all the loving things he said to me. Then I feel his love is still with me. Do you have any pictures of your mom, Anna?"

"I don't know where they are," I said.

"Maybe you can ask your Dad if you can have some pictures. Then you can put them in this book."

Mrs. Seasons walked to this chest, opened the drawer and took out a book. It had empty pages in it.

"Take the pictures and tape them in this book, Anna. You can write your thoughts and feelings next to the pictures. This will be your special memory book."

I liked this idea. If Mrs. Seasons does it, maybe I'll try it. So I took the book from Mrs. Seasons, picked up a pencil and wrote on the cover—Anna's Book.

⇢ My Secret ⇠

I wonder a lot about many things. Sometimes I wonder if my mom is watching me all the time. I wonder if she gets mad at me when I do something I'm not supposed to do, like playing with my computer instead of doing my homework. I wonder if she knows it's snowing out today.

One day I was sitting in Mrs. Seasons' big chair, eating my cookie, when I asked her something I wondered about for a long time, but was afraid to say it out loud to anyone.

"Mrs. Seasons?"

"Yes Anna."

Mrs. Seasons was always interested whenever she heard my voice.

"Mrs. Seasons, did you ever get mad at Frank?"

Mrs. Seasons put her head down and I could tell she was remembering something very hard. She rubbed her forehead and her eyes looked very sad. I listened to her answer very carefully.

"There was this one time, when Frank and I had this terrible argument. We both thought we were right and wouldn't give in. I was so angry with him. We said some hurtful things to each other because we were so angry. Have you ever gotten that angry at anyone, Anna?"

I felt very nervous now. My stomach was doing jumping jacks. I didn't know if I wanted to say what I was feeling. I was real scared. I looked at Mrs. Seasons and she had these warm eyes that said it was OK to say anything.

"One time, I got real mad at my mom. She wouldn't let me buy this shirt that I wanted. I thought she was so unfair and I told her so. But I also thought she was the worst mom ever. I'm glad I never said that but I still was thinking it. I feel so awful. I wonder if she thinks I don't love her."

"You know what I think, Anna?"

"What?" Anna wondered.

"I think you are a very brave girl for saying these feelings out loud. I think your mom would be very proud of you for speaking so honestly about the way you are feeling."

"Do you really think so?"

"Yes I do, Anna."

Now I felt a little bit better.

Later that day, I took my book, Anna's Book, and started to write to my mom. I talk to her a lot but this time I wanted to write a letter to her. I told her how much I missed her. But the real reason I wrote to her was to tell her how sorry I was for all the times I got mad at her, or didn't listen to her. I told her how much I loved her and wished I had said it every day, a thousand times a day. I cried a whole lot. When I finished, I took my book and hid it in my chest of drawers under my sweaters. I didn't want anyone to see it. Only I would know what I wrote. It was safe there.

⇢ Snowflakes ⇠

There have been a lot of gray skies these days. Everything looks dark. Sometimes it looks like it is going to rain or snow. When it looks dreary out, I wonder what I would be doing if my mom were here. What would we be talking about? Would we be going shopping? Would I like school more or would I be getting better grades?

One day, it was snowing out and I decided to go outside and play. It was one of those beautiful snow days. It wasn't cold from the wind. The snowflakes were big and beautiful, falling through the air like dancers. I tried to catch them on my sleeve. I could see them briefly and then they would disappear. I loved doing this, trying to catch them but they would always disappear. I then decided to make a snow angel. I fell on the snow, stretched my arms and legs as far as they could go. And then, swish, swish, up and down, up and down. I wanted to make a perfect snow angel. I tried to get up carefully to look at it and lost my balance. I fell right smack into the snow angel, messing up my design and getting my face and ears all cold. This was not fun anymore. I wondered why things never turn out the way I want them to.

I got up and walked to Mrs. Seasons' house. She was shoveling her walkway.

"What a great snow, Anna! Have you been playing in it?"

"Yes I have, Mrs. Seasons. I was making snow angels and I was also trying to catch snowflakes. Nothing turned out the way I wanted. The snowflakes disappeared and my snow angel turned out awful because I tripped and fell on it."

Mrs. Seasons walked over to me with the shovel in her hand. She took her hand and rubbed my back. Then she picked up a handful of snow and said,

"Look Anna. Look at the snowflakes."

I looked at the snow in her hand. I could

see some snowflakes but it also looked like one big snowball.

"What am I looking for Mrs. Seasons?"

"That's a real good question, Anna. Sometimes we get confused about what we are looking for. I know after my Frank died, nothing seemed right. I would forget things. I felt confused a lot and found myself looking for Frank, waiting for him to come home. I didn't want to change anything in the house. I wanted everything to be the same...kind of like the snowflakes... I didn't want them to disappear. Now I feel better. I've changed things in the house. I can go places by myself and feel OK. But this comes slowly. I know you miss your mom, Anna. And it must hurt you a lot."

I wondered how Mrs. Seasons knew I was missing my mom. I never said I was missing her. But I knew she was right. I think of her a lot. And I want her here with me right now.

"Mrs. Seasons, I want my mom here. I do miss her a lot."

"Anna, close your eyes and lift your head up to the sky."

I did what Mrs. Seasons asked me to do.

"Now open your eyes slowly."

The snow was falling all around me. I liked the feeling of being in the middle of snowflakes.

"Look at the beauty of the snowflakes, Anna. If we capture them, they disappear."

"I know," I sighed, "but I want them to stay."

Mrs. Seasons nodded. "That's the hard part. Life is changing all the time and we want to slow it down, hurry it up or stop it. What will never change, Anna, is your mom's love for you and your love for her. That love is forever."

I closed my eyes again, fighting back tears. When I opened my eyes, I looked up again. There I was, surrounded by dancing snowflakes, each one whispering *I love you* as they touched me and then disappeared.

❖ Dawn ❖

One Saturday morning I woke up and turned around in my bed to look out the window. I was so surprised. There were pink ribbons in the blue sky. I hadn't seen such a pretty sky in such a long time. Everything has been so gray for so long. Before, I would have yelled for my mom to come and see this beautiful sky. She would have sat on my bed and told me about the pretty skies she had seen. I would have smiled and begged her to tell me more stories. I really miss those times.

So I started to think about whom I could share this sky with or whether I wanted to share it with anyone. I had to decide quickly because the sky would change and it would just be blue again—not that there is anything wrong with a blue sky.

"Dad," I yelled. I shocked myself. What happens if he doesn't come, I wondered.

"Anna, where are you?"

"I'm in my room. Hurry, come see something."

My dad came through the doorway and I pointed to the window. He walked to the side of my bed and sat down.

"Isn't it beautiful," I said. "I thought you would miss it. You know how quickly things change."

"I'm really glad you called me, Anna."

My dad then held my hand and put his other arm around my shoulder. I loved when my dad held me. I felt safe.

"I would have missed this extraordinary sky and I would have missed sitting with you."

I wanted to tell him how sad I've been and how much I missed the old times—the times when all of us were together, when mom was here. But I just sat next to him feeling safe.

"Anna, I really miss your mom. It's been very hard for me. I also know you miss her deeply. You can come to me anytime you want to talk about mom, or cry, or just want to be close."

"Dad, I have something I want to show you." I got off my bed and went to my chest and opened up the bottom drawer. I reached underneath my sweaters and found my book—Anna's Book.

"Look, Dad. I found some pictures of mom and pasted them in here. I've also been writing to her about things. Mrs. Seasons gave me this idea. I really like it."

My dad carefully opened the book. He looked at the pictures. I could see him smile. I didn't want to make him sad. I didn't know how he felt about talking about mom.

"This is so wonderful, Anna. I wonder if this would help me?"

"It helped me because I can remember things we used to do together. I also like to see mom's face. Mrs. Seasons says my mom's love is all around me. This book helps me remember that."

My dad gave me a big hug.

"You've helped me very much this morning, Anna. I love you so much. My love will never change, even when I'm sad, angry or busy. Thank you for sharing your special book with me."

It was the first time I really talked to my dad about my mom. I'm really glad I did.

⇢ Choices ⇠

School, school, school. I hate it. I hate it. Why do we have to do these crazy things like projects or reports? They're stupid. I hate them. And the kids in my classroom...they ask stupid questions and say stupid things. I wish I didn't have to see them.

I knocked on Mrs. Seasons' door. I didn't feel like ringing her stupid cat doorbell. In fact, it felt good to bang on the door. Mrs. Seasons opened the door and invited me in.

"Hi Anna," Mrs. Seasons said.

"Hi," I answered.

"What's going on?"

"Not much."

Mrs. Seasons offered me cookies. I didn't feel like talking and I almost didn't feel like eating cookies.

"Thanks," I said half-heartedly.

"Want to sit in the living room?"

"Not really, Mrs. Seasons. I just want to walk around. I don't feel like sitting."

I was eating and walking, eating and walking. Mrs. Seasons was sitting by the kitchen table. I felt like I was going to jump out of my skin.

"I hate them all," I yelled. I startled myself. Mrs. Seasons looked at me. She didn't seem upset or angry. She just looked at me.

"I really hate them! I repeated. Why do they say such stupid things?"

"You sound angry, Anna." Mrs. Seasons sounded concerned.

"I'm not angry. I'm really mad."

"What happened that made you so mad, Anna?"

"The kids at school. They made me mad."

"All of them?" Mrs. Seasons wondered.

"Well, not all of them," I said.

"Anna, did someone say something that upset you?"

I didn't want to look at Mrs. Seasons. I put my head down. This was hard to say out loud.

"Some kids said I couldn't make a Mother's Day card because my mom was

dead. What do they know? Who told them anyhow? If I want to make a Mother's Day card, I can do it. No one can tell me what to do!"

"You're right, Anna. You can make a card if you want to."

I didn't know what to say. I felt this hurt right in my chest. I started to cry and couldn't stop for a long time. Mrs. Seasons walked me to the couch in the living room. We sat together for a long time, not saying very much. Mrs. Seasons held my hand the whole time. And I let her. I sat there, looking at the lines and wrinkles on Mrs. Season's hand. I wondered how hands change. When do those lines and wrinkles come? Is it from the sun or garden work?

Mrs. Seasons has a scar on her knuckle. I wonder how she got that. Did she cry? Was she alone when she cut her finger or was her mom there to help her?

I remembered my mom's hands. Her hands were not as wrinkly as Mrs. Seasons' but not as smooth or soft as mine. My mom's fingers were long and thin. She used to call them artist's fingers. My dad would say they looked like they were dancing whenever they would move, in perfect timing with life. I always wished I had her hands instead of mine. My fingers are short. They look so clumsy. My mom would always rub my hand when she would read to me. It felt so good, like two people who talk without saying words.

I wonder what my hands will look like when I'm older. Will they look wrinkly? Will my knuckles have scars on them? Will someone want to hold my hand?

Is this what happens when someone's heart gets hurt? Does it wrinkle up and show scars or can it stay soft as a pillow, like when I would lie on my mother's chest?

☞ The Promise ☜

Mrs. Seasons and I were sitting one day, talking about friends. We discussed what was important in choosing a friend and what we talk about with only our good friends.

"How is Julie?" Mrs. Seasons asked.

Mrs. Seasons met Julie one day last summer. Julie and I were jumping rope together and Mrs. Seasons was our audience. She even kept score for us. I think we also played hopscotch, a game Mrs.

Seasons played with one of her friends a long time ago.

"She's fine," I answered.

"Do you see her often?"

"Sometimes. Sometimes I feel like seeing her a lot and sometimes I don't."

"What does it depend on?" Mrs. Seasons wondered.

"I guess it's the way I'm feeling." I waited a few minutes to see if Mrs. Seasons would say anything. Sometimes she asks me questions and I just answer. But this time she didn't say anything. So I continued.

"Sometimes when I'm sad and I miss my mom, I feel funny talking to Julie about it because she has a mom."

"Why does that make you feel funny?"

"Because I'm not sure she would understand what it's like not to have a mom because her mom is around all the time. She can talk to her anytime she wants to. How could she understand?"

"People surprise us sometimes, Anna. Has she ever disappointed you or not been a friend to you?"

"No, I don't think so."

"Well, maybe you could give her the chance to understand you, Anna. You would also receive something."

"What's that, Mrs. Seasons?"

"A gift that grows more precious as you grow older—a dear friend."

I thought a lot about whether I was going to talk to Julie about my feelings.

I'm seeing her this Saturday. I'll just wait to see how it goes.

Saturday came and Julie and I decided to spend some time drawing. We were up in my room. I was on my bed, and Julie was sitting at my desk. We were talking about school and homework. We get way too much! I sat there, looking at Julie, wondering if she thinks I'm different than I used to be.

"Julie?" I asked.

"Yeah," Julie replied.

"Do you think I act any differently than I used to?"

"When?" Julie looked at me, wondering what these questions were all about.

"I don't know. Do you think I look or

act different than I used to, since last summer?"

"Do you mean since ...?"

"Yes, since my mom died," I interrupted.

"I don't think you're any different. You're still my friend." Julie said, still looking puzzled.

I was feeling relieved that something didn't change in my life. I still had my best friend.

"Do you think of my mom, Julie?"

"Every time I come here I think of her. I loved the flowers in your kitchen window. Your house always felt happy and warm."

"I felt funny talking to you about my mom, Julie. I wasn't sure you would want to hear about how I felt."

"If I had something awful happen to me, Anna, I would come and tell you. You are my best friend."

"I know. But this felt different."

"It's not different. Best friends stick by each other, no matter what. So, promise me that you will tell me when something is bothering you. Promise?"

"OK," I said.

"Let's make a heart promise, Anna. Let's both make pictures of our hearts. I'll draw your heart and you draw mine. Then we'll promise to protect each other's hearts. We'll keep our pictures in a safe and special place."

Julie took her colored pens out and I got my pencils. Julie started drawing my heart with beautiful shades of red. She drew a tiny teardrop falling from my heart, all filled with colors of the rainbow. Julie said, "when the sun shines on tears, a rainbow comes." I looked at Julie again. She truly was my best friend. I then asked if I could borrow her colored pens. I wanted to draw her beautiful heart. And for the first time, in a long time, I felt life would be OK.

P.S. I feel a little older now. Sometimes I feel like I know things about life that other kids don't know: I know that when you think life is going along just great, something can happen that changes everything. I thought I would never be happy again but now I am…sometimes. I know that my memories are important, even the ones that make me feel sad and uncomfortable.

I have a very best friend. I have a Dad, a brother and sister who love me and are also going through their own sadness.

But what I really know for sure is… I remember Mrs. Seasons with special love. One of the first things she said to me when I was eating cookies, sitting in her big chair was… "Sometimes things feel different after we sit with them for awhile." I think that's true. I think I am going to get a big chair in my room in case I need it. When I sit in it, trying to figure out my problems, I'll remember the things Mrs. Seasons said to me. She said nature leaves us many gifts to discover. She helped me remember that my Mom's love will never be taken from me. This love will always be with me, even when I am not thinking of her.

And most important, I'm thankful that she sat and listened to me, a little girl, who thought she was alone but came to realize she was surrounded by love.

"The Big Chair's narrator, Anna, explores the changes in her life after her mother's death. Her questions, feelings and fears may help other children find meaning when a loved one dies."

—Donna L. Schuurman, EdD, CT
National Director
The Dougy Center for Grieving
Children and Families,
Portland, Oregon

"The Big Chair is a metaphorical masterpiece exploring a young girl's grief journey as she is coping with the loss of her mother. Anna's sense of comfort and security in Mrs. Seasons' wisdom-filled answers regarding life, loss and love is nothing short of enduring and heart warming. These clearly conveyed messages Rotondo so skillfully articulates, is a captivating reminder that love continues on."

—Amy Quinlan, M.A.
Bereavement Coordinator,
Seasons of Life Hospice

"The Big Chair is a remarkably warm, soothing, yet honest book that is sure to soften the grief of any child or even adult who reads it. It invites readers to climb up with Anna into Mrs. Seasons' chair to surround themselves with her wisdom and comfort in sorting through the myriad of feelings associated with loss. What a gentle companion to any grieving child."

—Cyndi Jones
Founder of the Wildflower Camp Foundation,
serving grieving children.

"Beth Rotondo's story about Anna touches your heart. We can feel the comfort of sitting in Mrs. Seasons' big chair. The story is told with remarkable sensitivity to the worries and fears grieving children carry with them after a loss. Through Anna's relationship with Mrs. Seasons, the book helps us appreciate what makes grieving children feel safe and secure again."

—Elaine Devine, LICSW
Brigham and Women's Hospital

"Ms. Rotondo's book captures the essence of a young child's struggle with the grief process. Throughout the book, she beautifully illustrates typical reactions and changes children often experience after the death of a parent in a way that is often missed in storybooks written for children dealing with loss and grief. It normalizes the grief process in a way that allows children to understand that their grief journey is unique, but that the feelings and changes they experience are normal and natural responses to loss. This book also shows how important it is for adults to gently companion a child who is grieving, allowing them to trust their own ability to walk through their grief with new insights and confidence."

—Cindy Clark, MSW, CCLS
Owner of Hoping Skills Company
Sympathy Gift & Resource Center

For more information on
Threads of Hope,
an Offering for Those Who Grieve,
and
The Big Chair,
a Story of Grief and Discovery,
please email:
bethrotondo@verizon.net